W9-CTN-913

This book belongs to:

Milly

A catalogue record for this book is available from the British Library

Published by Ladybird Books Ltd
80 Strand, London, WC2R 0RL
A Penguin Company

2 4 6 8 10 9 7 5 3 1
© LADYBIRD BOOKS LTD MMIX
LADYBIRD and the device of a Ladybird are trademarks of Ladybird Books Ltd

ISBN: 978-1-40930-243-8

Printed in Italy

The Trouble with Thomas Tiger

written by Mandy Ross
illustrated by Jill McDonald

Every morning, as the sun rose over the jungle, Thomas Tiger would yawn and let out a huge *growl*!

GROWL!

Thomas's friends liked his morning growl because it woke them up before the sun got too hot.

Emma Elephant's breakfast grass was still soft and dewy. Hannah Hippo's mud was still nice and cool, and Gary Gorilla's favourite dozing spot was still leafy and shady – perfect!

But, one morning, as the sun rose over the jungle, Thomas woke up, yawned, and… nothing came out!

"Oh, no!" he whispered.
"I've lost my growl!"

With no special morning growl, everyone in the jungle slept late. By the time they got up, the sun was high in the sky.

Hannah's mud pool was boiling. Emma's grass was dry and hard. Gary's favourite dozing spot was hot and scratchy.

12

Everyone was miserable, especially Thomas.
"We've got to do something," said Emma.
"If we don't help Thomas to get his growl
back, we'll never wake up on time again."

15

"Let's play him some music," said Gary.
"Thomas might join in with a growl."

So Gary clapped some coconut shells
together. *Clippety-clop!*
Hannah bubbled water. *Bubbly-bop!*
And Emma drummed on a hollow
tree trunk. *Rum-a-dum-dum!*

*Clippety-clop, bubbly-bop,
rum-a-dum-dum!*

Thomas opened his mouth to growl...
but nothing came out!
"It's no good," he said, "my growl
has gone."
Poor Thomas! He sadly tucked his
tail between his legs.

"Let's try to make him laugh," said Hannah. "That might bring his growl back."

She swung on a vine and crashed into a tree.

THUNK!

Gary slipped on a banana skin and fell into the mud pool.

SPLOSH!

Emma tripped over a log and landed
on her bottom.

SPLAT!

It was all very silly.

Thomas opened his mouth to growl
with laughter… but nothing came out!
"It's no good," he said, sadly. "I have
to get used to being growl-free."
And with that, he sloped off,
curled up tight and went to sleep.

Suddenly, Emma had an idea...

"I know just the thing to bring Thomas's growl back," she said. "Follow me." She crept behind the rock where Thomas was sleeping.

"After three," said Emma. "Ready? One, two, *three*!"

They all jumped out with a super-loud
trumpety-growly-gurgly-bellow!
Thomas nearly jumped out of his skin.
He got such a fright that he opened
his mouth and let out the most
enormous *growl!*

"Hooray!" they all cheered.
"Thomas has found his growl!"

GRROWL!

From then on, nobody worried about sleeping late ever again. Their little growling alarm clock made sure of that.

GROWL!